For my father

Balzer + Bray is an imprint of HarperCollins Publishers
Little Penguin Stays Awake
Copyright © 2018 by Tadgh Bentley
All rights reserved. Manufactured in China.
No part of this book may be used or reproduced in any manner whatsoever without written permission except in the case of brief quotations embodied in critical articles and reviews. For information address HarperCollins Children's Books, a division of HarperCollins Publishers, 195 Broadway, New York, NY 10007.
www.harpercollinschildrens.com

ISBN 978-0-06-268977-1

The artist used pen and ink colored digitally to create the illustrations for this book.
Typography by Dana Fritts
18 19 20 21 22 SCP 10 9 8 7 6 5 4 3 2 1
❖
First Edition

Tadgh Bentley

Little Penguin Stays Awake

BALZER + BRAY
An Imprint of HarperCollinsPublishers

Oh, hello! I don't suppose you've seen any shooting stars this evening?

I have a very important wish—YAWN!— and I need a shooting star to make it come true.

You see, we penguins are very good at swimming and waddling and eating chili.

But there's one thing we can't do—fly.

I've always dreamed of spreading my
flippers and flying with my friends.
If I wish on a shooting star, my dream
HAS to come true!
There's just one problem. . . .

very early bedtimes

And shooting stars don't come out until late at night.

I've never stayed up this late before,
and I'm not sure I can do it.

chill

Kenneth and Franklin have tried all
sorts of things to keep me awake,

but nothing has worked.

So now—

YAWN!

—maybe YOU can help!

If you see me fall asleep, shout,

WAKE UP, LITTLE PENGUIN!

Now, you can't go to sleep without closing your eyes . . . so I've decided I'm not going to close mine.

Not even to blink or anything.

Ready?

Open your eyes wide . . .

wider . . .

wiiider. . . .

Don't blink—

SNORE!

WAKE UP, LITTLE PENGUIN!

Hmmm, maybe a little exercise will do the trick.

Let's try some **stretches!**

Stretch your flippers up high.

Stretch them to the side.

Stretch . . . far . . .

down . . . low. . . .

SNORE!

WAKE UP, LITTLE PENGUIN!

ARRGH!

The shooting stars are still nowhere
in sight, and I don't think I can stay
awake much longer!
What should we try next?

Maybe jumping jacks
will wake me up!

One 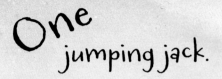 jumping jack.

Two 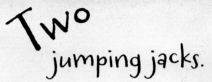 jumping jacks.

Three . . .

jumping . . . jacks.

SNORE!

WAKE UP, LITTLE PENGUIN!

Kenneth! Franklin!
The stars! They're here!
I made it! Oh, thank you
ever so much!

Now I can finally . . .

FINALLY . . .

make . . . my . . .

wish. . . .